D0595469

The Mystery of the Copycat Clown

Elspeth Campbell Murphy
Illustrated by Joe Nordstrom

BETHANY HOUSE PUBLISHERS
MINNEAPOLIS, MINNESOTA 55438

The Mystery of the Copycat Clown
Copyright © 1996
Elspeth Campbell Murphy

Cover and story illustrations by Joe Nordstrom

THREE COUSINS DETECTIVE CLUB® is a registered
trademark of Elspeth Campbell Murphy.

Scripture quotation is from the International Children's Bible.

Published by Bethany House Publishers
A Ministry of Bethany Fellowship, Inc.
11300 Hampshire Avenue South
Minneapolis, Minnesota 55438

Printed in the United States of America.

Library of Congress Cataloging-in-Publication Data

CIP applied for.

ELSPETH CAMPBELL MURPHY has been a familiar name in Christian publishing for over fifteen years, with more than seventy-five books to her credit and sales reaching five million worldwide. She is the author of the best-selling series *David and I Talk to God* and *The Kids From Apple Street Church*, as well as the 1990 Gold Medallion winner *Do You See Me, God?* A graduate of Trinity College and Moody Bible Institute, Elspeth and her husband, Mike, make their home in Chicago, where she writes full time.

Contents

1. The Clown Next Door 9
2. Picture of a Clown 12
3. Missing 15
4. A Puzzle 19
5. A Clown Named Phil 22
6. Stooges 26
7. Clown Cousins 30
8. The T.C.D.C. 34
9. Sammy W. 36
10. Sammy's Clown 39
11. Big Footprints 42
12. The Other Clown 45
13. Questions 48
14. Answers 52
15. Good Medicine 55

A happy heart is like good medicine.
But a broken spirit drains your strength.

Proverbs 17:22

1

The Clown Next Door

*T*itus McKay's father sighed deeply and shook his head. "I'm telling you, kids. That guy in the apartment next door is a real clown."

Titus groaned.

His little dog, Gubbio, yelped.

But his cousins, Timothy Dawson and Sarah-Jane Cooper, who were visiting, looked at their uncle in surprise. It didn't sound like a very nice thing to say about a neighbor.

"Why? What does he do?" asked Timothy.

"He's a clown," said Titus.

"Yes," said Sarah-Jane. "Uncle Richard just told us that. But what does he do?"

"He's a clown," said Titus.

"Right," said Timothy. "But what —?"

9

"He's a *clown!*" cried Titus a little desperately.

His father wasn't helping any. He just sat there laughing.

Titus took a deep breath and tried again. "He's a clown. It's what he does. It's his job."

His cousins stared at him.

Titus gave them a minute to think about it.

Finally Sarah-Jane said, "You mean he's a *real* clown? The guy in the apartment next door is a *real* clown?"

"Yes!" exclaimed Titus.

"Woof!" agreed Gubbio.

"Now I'm confused," said Titus's father. "What do you mean he's a *real* clown? I thought he was just some guy dressed up in a clown costume."

This time Sarah-Jane and Timothy groaned. Uncle Richard did that to you.

But they still wanted to hear more about the clown.

"He goes to clown school," their uncle told them.

"Oh, yeah, right," said Timothy, who was not going to be fooled again.

"No!" cried Titus as his father just sat and

grinned at Timothy. "My dear old dad isn't kidding this time. There really *is* a clown school! It's part of the theater department at the university where Dad teaches. Phil—that's our neighbor—takes classes there. Then he comes home and practices on me. He's really good! He's starting to get some odd jobs already."

"Well, of course they're *odd* jobs," said his father. "The guy's a *clown!*"

This time they all groaned.

11

2

Picture of a Clown

"So. When do we get to meet this Phil?" asked Timothy a little while later.

"Today," said Titus. "He's going to be working at the Children's Hospital fundraising picnic. My mom was on the planning committee. So we'll all be going."

"Sounds like fun," said Sarah-Jane. "I've never met a real clown before."

Titus could tell by the looks on his cousins' faces that they still weren't sure there even was a clown named Phil who lived next door.

Then Titus remembered something.

"Wait! I've got a picture of Phil and me. It was taken when he was doing a show at the Children's Hospital. Gubbio and I were there the same day as Phil, because it was Pet Day."

"*What* day?" asked Timothy.

"Pet Day," said Titus. "My parents and I are part of this program where people take their pets into hospitals. The idea is that pets cheer people up. Clowns do, too—which was why Phil was there. Anyway, when people are happy, they feel better.

"But not all dogs can do hospital visits, even with the special training. Some little dogs are just too yappy and crabby. Not Gubbio! He just loves people, don't you, boy? Especially kids. In fact, in the picture you'll see this little boy and his father in the background. The little boy is sitting in a wheelchair, and Gubbio is sitting on his lap. It's really cute."

Sarah-Jane picked up Gubbio and cuddled him. "Oh, you're just the sweetest little dog in the whole world, aren't you?"

Timothy stroked Gubbio's silky head. "You're just an all-around good dog, aren't you, boy?"

"Woof!" agreed Gubbio happily. He wasn't conceited or anything. But he wasn't going to argue, either.

While his cousins were making a fuss over his dog, Titus looked for the picture. His mother kept the family's favorite photographs on a table in the living room. They were all clustered together in a collection of pretty frames. Titus sorted through them for the picture of himself and Phil the Clown.

He couldn't find it.

3

Missing

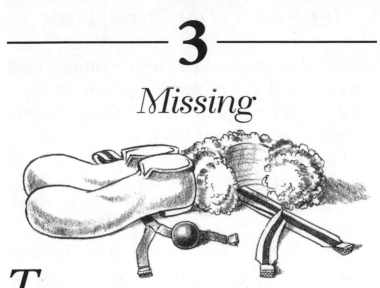

*T*imothy and Sarah-Jane didn't say anything. But they looked at him funny.

"Mom!" Titus called. "Where's that picture of Phil and me? You know—the one where he's all dressed up in his costume and clown makeup? I want to show it to Tim and S-J."

His mother answered from the kitchen. "It's right there on the table with all the other photographs."

"No, it isn't."

"Yes, it is."

"No, it isn't."

"Yes, it is."

"I can't find it."

"Look again."

Titus sighed. Why was it grown-ups always

said "look again" when you couldn't find something? Titus prided himself on doing a good job of looking in the first place. So why should he have to look again?

But he knew that a lot of detective work was just checking and double checking. Titus and his cousins had a detective club. They were very, very good at finding things.

Timothy and Sarah-Jane helped Titus to look again through the photographs on the table.

Then they checked the floor around the table. They looked under the floor-length tablecloth. They looked behind the sofa and chairs. Anywhere the photograph might have fallen.

They couldn't find it.

"Mom!" called Titus. "I'm telling you, it's not here."

"Aurggh!" roared his mother, coming out of the kitchen, wiping her hands on a towel. But it was a friendly roar, and she was smiling as she looked through the photographs herself.

"I *know* the picture is here, because I showed it to the people at the committee meeting. We talked about how some of the children from the hospital are going to be at the fundraising picnic. And since Phil has entertained at the hospital, we thought he should be at the fundraiser, too. Even old Mr. Witherspoon agreed. And he doesn't agree with much!"

"Who's Mr. Witherspoon?" asked Sarah-Jane.

"He's an older gentleman," her aunt told her. "He teaches acting at the university. And he does a lot of good committee work. It's just that he's kind of . . . well, he's sort of . . ."

Titus said, "Let's put it this way. If he were a little dog, he'd be the yappy, crabby kind."

His mother laughed. "I guess he would! I never thought of it like that. But often crabby people are actually just tired and sad. Unfortunately, they take out their upset feelings on other people."

"And then the *other* people end up being sad and crabby," said Timothy. "And they take it out on more people."

"Too true," said Aunt Jane. "That's why it's good to have clowns—to cheer everybody up."

"Maybe Phil will cheer up Mr. Witherspoon," said Sarah-Jane.

"That would be nice," replied her aunt.

"But Mr. Witherspoon said he wouldn't be able to come to the picnic today. It's too bad. It would do him good to be with the children. There was a quarrel years ago in his family. He has a grown son who lives in the area. But Mr. Witherspoon has never even met his grandchild."

The cousins looked at one another in disbelief. Their own grandparents drove around with a bumper sticker that said: *Ask us about our grandchildren!!!* It was hard to believe anyone could have a grandchild nearby that he had never even met.

All this time, Mrs. McKay had been sorting through the photographs on the table, looking for the one of Titus and Phil. At last she said, "That's odd! Where could it be?"

4

A Puzzle

Titus's mother glanced at her watch and headed back to the kitchen.

"Well, that certainly is a puzzle! But I can't stop to look for it now. I have to get these cookies ready for the picnic, and I'm running late. I'm sure the picture will turn up."

That was another thing grown-ups always said when you couldn't find something. Titus didn't know if they actually believed it or not. But in his experience as a detective, things didn't just walk away. And they didn't just turn up.

"What could have happened to it?" he wondered aloud.

Timothy said, "Maybe Uncle Richard took

it with him when he went to the office a little while ago."

Titus said, "He already has pictures of Mom and me there. But it's worth checking that out."

He called his father and asked him about the picture. It wasn't at the office. And his father hadn't moved it from its regular place at home. He hadn't even known it was missing.

Sarah-Jane said, "Your mom said she showed it to people at the committee meeting. Maybe someone was looking at it and put it back in the wrong place."

Titus said, "That makes sense, too. But then the picture would still be somewhere in the living room—just in the wrong place. And it seems that my parents or I would have come across it by now."

Just to be sure, they looked around the living room and even the rest of the apartment. They didn't think they would find it. And they were right. They didn't.

Titus said, "Maybe somebody absent-mindedly took it home after the meeting."

Timothy said, "It's possible. But it seems to me you would notice if you were carrying around somebody else's framed picture."

Sarah-Jane said, "You would certainly notice the picture when you got home and put your own stuff away. Then you would call to apologize. And you would bring the picture back right away."

Titus said, "Maybe Phil borrowed it. But no—that doesn't make sense, either. The picture came out really well. So my parents had a copy made for Phil. He wouldn't have to borrow ours. Besides, Phil wouldn't take something without asking first."

"Who would?" asked Timothy.

"And why?" asked Sarah-Jane.

Titus shook his head. It certainly was a puzzle.

5

A Clown Named Phil

They were still puzzling over the missing photograph when there was a knock at the door.

"Kids, see who it is, will you?" called Titus's mother. "I'm up to my elbows here."

Titus peeped out. "It's Phil," he called back to his mother.

"Have him come in," she said. "I'll be there in a minute."

As Titus opened the door, he saw Timothy and Sarah-Jane glance excitedly at each other. At last they were going to meet the famous Phil.

Titus knew they were going to be disappointed. Phil wasn't in costume.

"Oh!" cried Sarah-Jane, when Titus had

introduced them. "I thought you would look like a clown. But you just look like a regular person."

"Actually," said Timothy. "You look like a tall Titus."

Titus and Phil looked at each other and burst out laughing.

Thin. Dark hair. Glasses.

Yes, they did look a lot alike.

Phil said, "I never noticed that before. But Timothy has just given me a great idea. I came over here to ask Titus to help me out at the fair today. You know, to be my assistant with the props and things. But how would it be if I painted you three up to look like me? We could be Big Clown, Little Clowns."

"EX-cellent!" said Titus.

"Neat-O!" said Timothy.

"So cool!" said Sarah-Jane.

"Speaking of face paint," said Titus. "You didn't happen to borrow that picture of you and me, did you, Phil?"

"No," said Phil. "I have my own copy. Why?"

Titus explained about not being able to find the picture.

"Hmmm," murmured Phil. "That *is* odd. But I'm sure it will turn up. In the meantime, let me run next door and get my copy. Maybe if your cousins see me in my get-up, they'll stop looking at me funny."

"Funny ha-ha? Or funny weird?" asked Timothy.

"Funny weird," said Phil, making a funny ha-ha face. "Back in a second."

And he was—with the photograph of himself and Titus.

"So!" said Sarah-Jane in a tone of voice that settled things. "You really are a clown."

"Yes," said Phil. "I really am. I spent a long time getting my costume and makeup just right. How I look as a clown is my trademark, you know."

"What does that mean?" asked Timothy.

Phil explained. "It means that clowns are like snowflakes—no two are exactly alike. Or at least they shouldn't be! You can get ideas from other clowns. But you're not supposed to copy them."

Titus said, "We can look like you, because we're going to be your assistants. But if anyone else looked exactly like you, he would be a copycat clown. And that's not allowed, right?"

"Right," said Phil. "There shouldn't be any copycat clowns."

6

Stooges

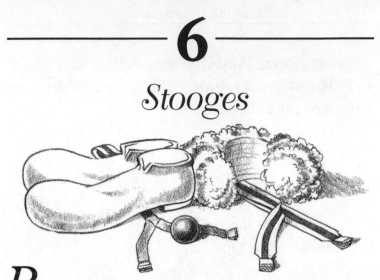

*P*hil said, "So it's settled. You guys will be my stooges today."

"Your *what*?" cried Timothy and Sarah-Jane together. They sounded as if they thought this day just couldn't get any stranger.

Titus laughed. "A stooge is the clown's assistant. He's the 'straight man.' He's the serious partner who helps the clown get laughs."

"Oh," said Sarah-Jane, trying to take this in.

Phil smiled at her. "You never can have too many stooges, I always say."

Titus said, "Yeah, except—there are *three* of us. So that would make us your—"

Just then Gubbio came over and joined their little group.

"My four stooges," said Phil. "I thought Gubbio could come along, too, if that's all right with you."

"It's fine with me," said Titus. "Being the four stooges is better than being the three stooges any day. But Gubbio doesn't know any tricks."

"Woof," agreed Gubbio. He didn't sound too upset about this.

Neither was Phil. He said, "Gubbio is so cute he doesn't need to do any tricks. He can just be there. The kids will know him from the hospital visits. And that will make them feel right at home. I even made a little dog ruffle to match my costume—if you think he would wear it. . . ."

Gubbio sniffed the ruffle suspiciously. But he let Titus try it on him. And—as Sarah-Jane put it—you could just die from cuteness.

"What do you want us to do?" asked Titus.

"Good question," replied Phil. "I had the day all planned out. But then I got a phone call telling me the schedule had been changed. I was planning to do a walk-around before the show. But now they want me to come later and just do the show first."

"What's a walk-around?" asked Sarah-Jane.

"It's pretty much what it sounds like," explained Phil. "The clown walks around through the crowd. Talking to people. Maybe handing out balloons. It gets people enthusiastic. It's a great way to get everyone ready for the show. I was surprised when the planning committee wanted to change that."

Just then Titus's mother came in. She looked at Phil in alarm. "My goodness, Phil! Why aren't you in costume?"

Phil said, sounding very puzzled, "It's like I was explaining to Titus and Timothy and Sarah-Jane. I got a phone call from someone on the committee telling me not to come until it's time for the show. I thought it was a little odd to have a change in plans like that. But the guy I talked to sounded very definite."

Titus's mother shook her head. "No. No, there was no change of plans. Who called you?"

"Mr. Browning," replied Phil. "A Mr. Stuart Browning."

Mrs. McKay plopped down on the nearest

chair and stared at Phil.

"Mom! What's the matter?" cried Titus.

"There's no one on the committee named Stuart Browning," she said.

7

Clown Cousins

*F*or a moment they all just sat there staring at one another. They were all thinking the same thing: What in the world was going on? No one had an answer for that question.

Then everyone seemed to remember at the same time how late it was getting. Suddenly there was a wild scramble to get ready. No time to figure anything out.

Phil rushed next door to put on his costume and makeup.

Timothy, Titus, and Sarah-Jane helped Mrs. McKay to pack the cookies for the picnic. And by the time the cousins were ready to go, Phil was back to paint their faces.

Phil worked quickly and carefully. He did a great job. The cousins looked at one another and burst out laughing.

There was something about having your face painted, Titus thought. It just made you feel funny. Not funny weird. Funny ha-ha.

Even though they were related, Titus and Timothy and Sarah-Jane didn't look all that much alike. But now they looked almost exactly alike. And they all looked just like Phil.

Phil stood back to admire his work.

"Perfect!" he declared. "And it's a good thing, too. I thought I needed your help before. But now with the crazy mix-up, I *really* need your help. I'll need some time to get the show set up. So you can do part of my walk-around for me. How would that be? I'll give you some balloons to pass out. And you can tell people where the show is and when to gather for it. Also, people will probably ask you about getting their faces painted, too. Tell them I'll be doing that after the show."

When it came to being a clown, Phil really seemed to know what he was doing.

Titus could tell his cousins were feeling the same way he was—wiggly with excitement. He snapped on Gubbio's leash, and they were off.

They were all a little breathless when they

finally got to the park where the picnic was being held. But they had made it in pretty good time after all.

Titus's father caught up with them there. He said something about poor Phil having to work with a bunch of clowns. And everyone groaned. Then Titus's parents hurried off to help get the food set up.

Phil began blowing up helium balloons in the same quick, careful way he had painted their faces.

Soon each cousin had a nice big bunch of gorgeous balloons. Titus thought he was going to fly away. Partly from those balloons. And partly from excitement.

They were just about to start off when a man came up and introduced himself to Phil. He was the head of the Children's Hospital.

"Sorry I didn't get a chance to talk to you earlier," said the man.

"No, I'm the one who should be sorry," began Phil. "I wasn't even *here* earlier. You see—"

But before he could explain, the man just laughed and said, "OK. I'll play along and pretend you just got here. That's a *great* trick, by the way. I don't know how you did it—getting from there to here so fast. But I know you can't give away your secrets. Now, if you'll excuse me, I have to say hello to those people over there. I only wish I could be in two places at once the way you can. It's a great trick!"

Phil and the cousins stood staring after him.

Then they all looked at one another and said, "What was he talking about? *What* trick?"

8

The T.C.D.C.

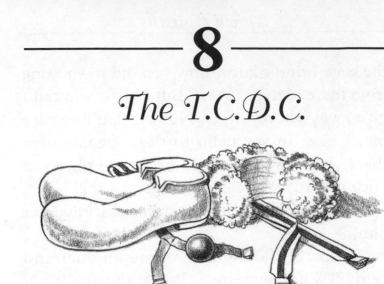

*P*hil said, "What did he mean that I didn't just get here? And what did he mean that I get around really fast? I came straight to the stage with you guys to blow up balloons. I haven't been anywhere else in the park.

"First it was that strange phone call. And now it's someone saying he likes my tricks—when I haven't done any tricks."

"Actually," said Timothy, "the first strange thing to happen was Ti's missing photograph."

Phil looked at them in surprise. "Do you really think that has anything to do with all this?"

Titus shrugged. "Maybe not. It's just that sometimes when a lot of strange things happen at the same time . . . well, is it really a coincidence?"

"Hmmm," Phil murmured, thinking this over. "Maybe you're right. But that doesn't give us any answers. It just makes things more complicated."

Sarah-Jane said, "Don't worry, Phil. You've always got the T.C.D.C."

But that just made Phil look even more puzzled. "What's a 'teesy-deesy'?" he asked.

"It's letters," explained Titus. "Capital T. Capital C. Capital D. Capital C. It stands for the Three Cousins Detective Club."

"Detectives, huh?" said Phil. "Do you think you could be detectives and clowns at the same time? That's not a bad cover when you come to think of it. You can help me with my walk-around just as we planned. But at the same time you can be looking around. See if you can figure out what's going on. No one will know what you're up to. And I'll catch up with you as soon as I can."

"You know," said Titus, "you're pretty smart for a clown."

Phil laughed and took a bow. "And may I say that you're pretty smart for a stooge."

9

Sammy W.

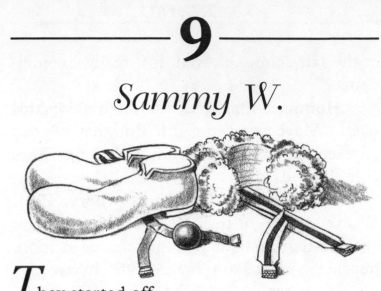

*T*hey started off.

Titus didn't know how much they would be able to find out as detectives. But one thing was sure: They were a big help for Phil's show! As soon as the other kids saw the cousins, they wanted balloons and painted faces, too. It was fun getting so much attention.

Even Gubbio seemed to be enjoying himself. He trotted along at Titus's side with the cute little clown ruffle around his neck.

Suddenly Gubbio stopped and perked up his ears.

At first the cousins couldn't hear anything. (A dog's hearing is better than a person's.) But then the cousins all heard it, too. Someone was calling to Gubbio by name.

Gubbio tugged at the leash. He wanted to go in the direction of the voice. Titus couldn't blame him. By that time his own curiosity was getting pretty worked up.

So Titus let Gubbio take the lead. And he, Timothy, and Sarah-Jane trotted along beside Gubbio rather that the other way around.

Gubbio led them through the crowds right over to where a little boy sat in a wheelchair.

"Gubbio!" cried the little boy. "I thought that was you!"

"Woof! Woof! Woof!" exclaimed Gubbio as if he had just met a long-lost friend.

The little boy was wearing a name tag that said *Sammy W.*

"How does Sammy know Gubbio?" asked Timothy.

Titus had been wondering the same thing. Suddenly it came to him. "Sammy must be one of the kids who plays with Gubbio in the hospital on Pet Day."

Sarah-Jane said, "That explains how Gubbio and Sammy know each other. But it doesn't explain why Sammy looks so familiar to *me*. I just *know* I've seen that little kid somewhere before."

"Me, too," said Timothy. "But where?"

Sammy clapped his hands. And Titus let go of the leash so that Gubbio could jump up on Sammy's lap.

"That's it!" cried Sarah-Jane. "That's where I've seen that little boy before. He's the one in the photograph."

10

Sammy's Clown

At first Titus couldn't understand what Sarah-Jane was talking about. "What photograph?" he asked. But before she could answer, he cried softly, "Oh! Oh! The picture of Phil and me! Sammy is the little boy in the background!"

"Exactly," said Sarah-Jane.

"Another coincidence?" asked Timothy.

"I don't know," said Titus. "I mean, there's no reason Sammy wouldn't be here. But even so . . ."

Sammy looked up from petting Gubbio and laughed. "You boys look like that clown!"

It wasn't that Sammy was ignoring Sarah-Jane. It's just that he was so excited by having big boys like Timothy and Titus pay attention to him.

Sarah-Jane offered to decorate Sammy's wheelchair with balloons, and he liked that idea a lot.

Titus said to him, "We *do* look like that clown, Sammy. You have a good memory. The clown's name is Phil. And he was at the hospital one time on Pet Day. That's where you saw him before."

Sammy shook his head. "Not just then. Today."

The cousins looked at one another in surprise.

"When was this?" asked Timothy.

"A long time ago," said Sammy.

Titus said carefully, "Well, that's right, Sammy. Phil *is* here today. I'm just surprised you saw him already. You see, he's busy getting ready for his show. But I know he would like to talk to you later."

This time Sammy nodded. "I know that. Because you know why? He already did."

"Already did what?" asked Timothy.

"Talked to me," said Sammy. "And he showed me magic tricks. I wanted him to stay and show my daddy. But the clown said he had to go see some other kids. But he said he would come back later and talk to me some more."

"Oh," said Titus. And that was all any of them could think of to say.

11

Big Footprints

*A*ll this time people had been bringing wheelchairs over for Sarah-Jane to decorate. Soon the cousins were out of balloons. So they decided to go back to get some more.

"What do you think about Sammy's clown?" Timothy asked Titus and Sarah-Jane when they had said goodbye to Sammy.

"Well," said Sarah-Jane, "I suppose it's possible Sammy made the whole thing up about talking to a clown. Little kids have big imaginations sometimes."

Titus said, "He may have made up the part about Phil talking to him and doing magic tricks. But I don't think he would have made up the part about a clown being at the picnic. He must have seen Phil somehow."

"When?" asked Timothy with a thoughtful frown. "Sammy said he talked to the clown a long time ago."

"Little kids can't keep track of time very well," said Sarah-Jane. "Maybe it just *seemed* like a long time ago to him." But she sounded as puzzled as Timothy.

Titus said, "There's only one way to find out if Phil is doing a walk-around already. And that's to go back to the stage and see if he's there. If he's not, we'll have to catch up with him to get some more balloons."

"He said he would catch up with us," Timothy pointed out. "And he hasn't."

Just then a bright spot of color on the ground caught Titus's eye. It was a fuzzy pompom button.

Titus knew it was from Phil's outfit. But there, beside it in the dirt, was even extra proof.

A footprint. A big footprint. A big, big, BIG footprint. A footprint so big, it could only have been made by a giant clown shoe.

Titus said, "Well, I guess that settles it. Phil must be out doing his walk-around. But let's take the pompom back to the stage so we don't

lose it. Maybe Phil will have time to sew it on before the show."

When the cousins got to the stage, they were surprised to see Phil there. He was chatting with a group of children.

The cousins were even more surprised to see every pompom on Phil's outfit neatly in place.

12

The Other Clown

*P*hil came over and greeted them with a big smile. "Hey! You guys have been doing a great job! People are so excited about the show that they've been coming to talk to me instead of me going to them."

"So you haven't been out on a walk-around?" asked Timothy.

"No," said Phil in surprise. "I haven't moved from this spot since we got here. Why do you ask?"

Titus held out the pompom. "We found this way over there." He pointed across the park.

Phil glanced down at his costume. "It doesn't seem to be mine," he said.

"No," said Titus. "I think it belongs to the other clown."

His cousins and Phil stared at him. "*What* other clown?" they cried.

"I know it sounds crazy," Titus said. "But just think about it. If Phil was here the whole time, then how did that big footprint get on the other side of the park? And who was talking to Sammy?"

"What footprint?" asked Phil, sounding thoroughly confused. "And who's Sammy?"

"He's a little boy in a wheelchair," explained Sarah-Jane. "He's wearing a name tag that says *Sammy W.* He was in the hospital when you did your show there. But he says you talked to him today, too. Here in the park. And that you showed him magic tricks."

Phil just shook his head.

Timothy said, "At first we thought Sammy was making things up. But then we found the pompom with a giant footprint beside it."

Titus was thinking out loud. "And it's not just Sammy who saw the other clown—if we're right that there is another clown. What about the hospital director? He thought Phil was here early. But actually Phil was here late."

"Because of the phone call," said Phil.

"Right," said Titus. "Because of the phone call. So who called you? And who was it the director saw earlier today?"

Timothy added, "The director thought it was a great trick that Phil could get from one place to another so fast. But Phil was never anywhere but here. So what we're saying is—"

Sarah-Jane picked up the thought. "It was never one clown in two places. It was two different clowns."

Phil said, "But the director thought this other clown was *me*. How could another clown look exactly like me?"

"A copycat clown," said Titus. "But we don't know how he did it."

"Still, I've got to hand it to you," said Phil. "You kids are really good detectives."

The cousins shrugged. They weren't conceited or anything. But they weren't going to argue with that.

"The problem is," Phil continued, "none of this makes any sense."

The cousins couldn't argue with that, either.

13

Questions

"So now what do we do?" asked Timothy.

It was a good question.

Titus tried to answer it. "We could go back to where we found the footprint. Maybe we'll find more and we can follow them."

It wasn't that good of an idea, and Titus knew it. The ground wasn't wet. And the park was mostly covered in grass anyway. There had just been that one small patch of dirt where they had found the footprint. There might be more prints. But Titus doubted it.

Then he thought of something else. "I think we'd better go tell my mom about this copycat clown. I mean, he might be a thief in disguise. He might be after the fundraising money."

Titus's parents were going to join them for the show. But the cousins thought it would be a good idea to go meet them on the way.

Phil agreed. "If you can help straighten things out, that would be great! My stooges are really working overtime today!"

"Woof!" said Gubbio. He liked to join in the conversation from time to time, even if he didn't know what was going on.

On the way to find Titus's parents, Sarah-Jane said, "I don't get it. If the copycat clown is a thief, why did he spend all that time being so nice to Sammy? Why not just take the money and run?"

Timothy said, "But if he's not a thief, why go to all the trouble of putting on a disguise? Why would someone dress up like a clown when he's not a clown?"

An idea was beginning to take shape in Titus's mind.

He said slowly, "He didn't just dress up like any old clown. That's because anyone on the committee would notice an extra, different-looking clown. But this guy dressed up like Phil. *Exactly* like Phil. If you saw him, you'd think he *was* Phil."

Sarah-Jane said, "But how would the copycat clown know what to wear? How would he know how to do his face?"

"Well," said Titus, "it would help if he had a picture to work from."

"*Your* picture?" asked Timothy. "The one of Phil and you? You think somebody wanted to dress up like a clown and steal money from the picnic? So he first broke into your apartment and stole the picture of you and Phil? How would he even know it was there?"

Titus said, "I think the copycat clown stole my picture, the one of Phil and me at the hospital. But he didn't have to break into my apartment to do it. And he's not here to steal the fundraising money."

"You're on to something, aren't you, Ti?" said Sarah-Jane. "What is it?"

"I'm not sure," said Titus. "But I think I know who the copycat clown is. And I think I know why he's here. I just have to ask Sammy one question. And then I'll know for sure."

Sammy and his father were on their way to see the show.

Before his cousins could ask him any more

50

questions, Titus dashed over to Sammy and whispered in his ear.

Then he ran back to his cousins.

"Well?" demanded Sarah-Jane.

"Well?" demanded Timothy. "What did you ask Sammy?"

Titus said, "I asked him about his name tag. I asked him what the *W* stands for."

14

Answers

*I*t took a while—quite a while—for the cousins to explain to Titus's parents about the copycat clown.

Titus said, "Just suppose for a minute that the photograph of Phil and me was stolen. Who could have taken it? Someone on the planning committee. That's the last time you remember seeing it, right?"

"That's true," said his mother.

Titus went on. "And who could have made the strange phone call to Phil, telling him to come later? Who could change the plans like that? It had to be someone who knew what the plans were in the first place. Someone on the planning committee."

"Let me get this straight," said his father.

"You're saying that someone stole the photograph in order to copy Phil's outfit? And then he called to keep Phil away so that he could take his place for a while?"

"That's right," said Titus.

"But *why?*" asked his father.

Titus said, "It was all because of Sammy."

Titus had to give his parents credit. They were really trying hard to listen and make sense of his wild-sounding story. He could see them take a deep breath.

"Who's Sammy?" they asked.

"He's the little boy in the photograph of Phil and me," explained Titus. "He's in the background—with Gubbio on his lap."

"Woof!"

"I remember him, of course," said Titus's mother. "But what—?"

"It was *Sammy* the copycat clown spent all that time with today. It was *Sammy* the clown came to see."

"Woof! Woof! Woof!"

Titus's mother said gently, "There's just one problem, sweetie. Everyone from the committee is here today. All looking like themselves."

"Not everyone," said Titus. "Someone told you he *wouldn't* be here today. But he was planning the whole time to come. And he did come. But not as himself. He came dressed up like Phil."

Timothy and Sarah-Jane had been bouncing up and down all this time, trying to keep quiet. The cousins all knew from experience that grown-ups listened better when only one kid talked at a time. This was Titus's story, and Timothy and Sarah-Jane wanted to let him tell it. But now they were ready to burst.

"Tell them about Sammy's name tag!" they said. "Tell them what the *W* stands for!"

"Woof! Woof! Woof! Woof! Woof!" said Gubbio.

"Witherspoon," said Titus.

15

Good Medicine

"Woof! Woof! Woof! Woof! Woof!"

Gubbio ran away with his leash and stood barking at a big nearby tree. What was it? Not even Gubbio could get that excited about birds and squirrels.

Out from behind the tree stepped—a *clown*.

"Mr. Witherspoon?!" gasped Titus's mother. "Mr. Witherspoon, is that you?"

"Yes," replied the clown. "I heard what these children were telling you. And they have it figured out right. I am the copycat clown. And little Sammy Witherspoon is my grandson. A grandson I have never seen in person—until today. I quarreled with his father—my son, that is—many years ago. We have not spoken in all that time."

Mr. and Mrs. McKay just nodded. They didn't ask him what the quarrel was about. Some things are private.

Mr. Witherspoon went on. "This quarrel with my son was much more my fault than his. I just—I just haven't known how to make it right.

"When I saw the photograph at the planning meeting, with my son and grandson in the background . . . well, I just couldn't stand it anymore. I knew I had to see Sammy. And I have—although I didn't tell him who I was."

Mr. Witherspoon gave a faint smile. "I have kept track of my family, though. I knew Sammy was in and out of the hospital for long-term treatment. So I thought there was a good chance he would be at the picnic today. But I didn't know how my son would react to seeing me. And I was afraid to find out. So what did I do? I dressed up like a clown in order to see my grandson. Maybe it's the perfect disguise for an old fool like me."

"There's nothing foolish about loving your kids," said Titus's father.

Mr. Witherspoon looked at him gratefully. "My plan was to get here early and just see Sammy from a distance. But I talked to him. And, well, for some reason, I just couldn't leave."

Titus's mother said, "I think you stayed because you wanted to talk to your son, too. Otherwise you could have left long ago, and no one would ever have known you were here."

"The question," said Mr. Witherspoon, "is whether my son wants to talk to *me*. I wouldn't blame him if he didn't want to. And, as I said, I'm afraid to find out."

"Then let me find out for you," said Mr. McKay. "Your son is watching the show with Sammy, right? Let me go talk to him and tell him what you've done today."

Mr. Witherspoon nodded. "All right. Please see if he'll talk to me."

After Mr. McKay left, there was an awkward silence. Then Titus thought of something to say.

"You teach acting, don't you, Mr. Witherspoon? That's how you knew about costumes and makeup."

"Quite right," the old man replied. "And it might interest you to learn that I also know a lot about clowns. As a young man, I ran away and joined the circus."

Naturally, the cousins wanted to hear all about *that*! Mrs. McKay said they'd better not get any ideas.

Then they all looked up and saw Sammy's wheelchair in the distance with all its bright balloons bobbing in the breeze.

Mr. McKay was pushing Sammy.

But Mr. Witherspoon's son was not with them.

That's because he was way out ahead of them, running toward his father with his arms open wide.

As soon as Mr. McKay and Sammy caught up with Sammy's father and grandfather, Titus's family tiptoed away. Some things are private.

The show was still going on, and they found some empty seats way in back.

Titus picked up his brilliant little dog and put him on his lap.

Phil was doing a great job. The audience loved him. They were laughing like crazy.

But Titus's father had a serious look on his face. He leaned over to the cousins as if he had something amazing and important to tell them.

He nodded toward Phil and whispered, "Do you see that guy up there? Well, guess what I found out. He's a *real clown!*"

Everyone else in the audience was laughing.

But the cousins just groaned.

The End

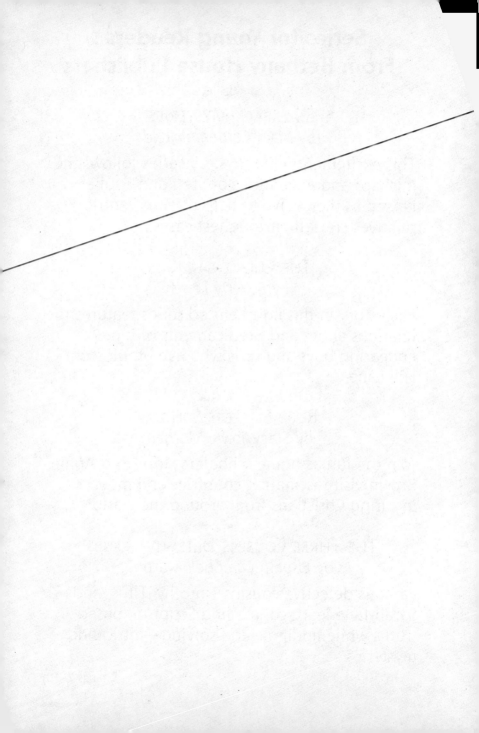

Series for Young Readers*
From Bethany House Publishers

★ ★ ★

BACKPACK MYSTERIES
by Mary Carpenter Reid

This excitement-filled mystery series follows the mishaps and adventures of Steff and Paulie Larson as they strive to help often-eccentric relatives crack their toughest cases.

★ ★ ★

THE CUL-DE-SAC KIDS
by Beverly Lewis

Each story in this lighthearted series features the hilarious antics and predicaments of nine endearing boys and girls who live on Blossom Hill Lane.

★ ★ ★

RUBY SLIPPERS SCHOOL
by Stacy Towle Morgan

Join the fun as home-schoolers Hope and Annie Brown visit fascinating countries and meet inspiring Christians from around the world!

★ ★ ★

THE THREE COUSINS DETECTIVE CLUB®
by Elspeth Campbell Murphy

Famous detective cousins Timothy, Titus, and Sarah-Jane learn compelling Scripture-based truths while finding—and solving—intriguing mysteries.

* (ages 7–10)

9608